HANNA'S BUTTERFLY

WRITTEN BY
MARIE VINJE

ILLUSTRATED BY
GAIL L. SUESS

One day in the park
Hanna found a butterfly
resting on the ground.

She picked it up with care
and wondered why it was there.

It had dots and stripes
of many kinds with bright
colors and curving lines.

She took it home and
asked her mother why
the little butterfly did not fly.

Her mother said it may have been hurt by the wind and rain and needed to rest.

So Hanna put leaves
in an empty jar to make
a butterfly nest.

That night as Hanna lay in bed, she thought about what her mother had said.

Some butterflies fly many miles
at the end of summer
to places that are warmer.

MOURNING CLOAK

PAINTED LADY

MONARCH

Migration

For this one to make the trip,
it could not wait much longer.

In the morning Hanna was happy to see her butterfly spread its wings out wide.

It needed more room to move
and wanted to be outside.

Hanna took the butterfly back to the park and sat down under a tree.

She lifted the lid off the jar
and let her friend go free.

It rested for a moment on a nearby plant. Hanna wondered if it would leave.

But then it fluttered its beautiful wings and lifted off into the breeze.